The Uneasy

Andrew Hook

The Uneasy
by Andrew Hook

ISBN: 978-1-908125-71-2

Cover Art by David Rix

Publication Date: March 2019

All text copyright 2019 Andrew Hook

Imogen was reminded of a science experiment where she had to depress the bulb of a pipette as it was immersed in blue ink. Releasing her grip drew the liquid into the thin tube. She held it carefully, transported the colour across to a clear glass of water, then released a drop with a light squeeze and watched the ink break the surface shine like a diver in a navy-blue costume disintegrating upon impact.

Gradually, the ink merged with the water; firstly like a squid ejecting fluid to repel an enemy with the colour resembling the actual shape of a squid as it dispersed; and secondly a process much more subtle until the transformation was complete and the clear glass contained a light blue liquid with the boundaries between the two substances now impossible to discern.

It was thus how she imagined her descent from normalcy into surrealism since her arrival in Paris; a gradual immersion into a different coloured world.

Imogen came to Paris believing it to be the city of romance and love – of starlit clichés – yet hadn't considered that it had also been surrealism's birthplace. François was to tell her that many surrealist artists met at 54, Rue Du Chateau, where they performed the first *cadavers exquis* in 1926, and that the building had since been demolished. But it was a while before she would meet him. Today we capture her solo, the morning after she has discovered the apartment within which she will permanently reside.

The room had been let by an inquisitive woman in a brown chemise and pleated skirt fronting a four-storey boarding house within which Imogen now had the highest view. Gulls flickered at the peripheries of her vision, wingtip white. Imogen had work in the perfumery industry: her turnout was impeccable. She was used to fabulous clients and intimations of wealth and whilst her personal planet skirted the peripheries of the galaxy she was drawn in by the bright stars and could glimpse their circular orbits, becoming close enough to approximate a touch.

The ground floor of the building housed a café with three rows of bottles strafing shelving on the back wall, upended and plugged. Circular tables had red and black chequered cloths thrown over them as though they had arrived by parachute. Imogen made it her ritual to order a morning coffee, the liquid as dark as the caves of Lascaux. Using a pipette, she placed one drop of cream into its centre, watched it disperse like a negative photograph of a Rorschach test or a pupil exposed to sunlight.

She favoured the use of the pipette as she believed it lent her a mysterious air.

The pipette had been borrowed from her scientist brother. An unknown swap.

Imogen sought to reinvent herself in fresh surroundings, to add quirks and eccentricities that would have felt odd on the other side of La Manche. She was an open book, a palimpsest. She identified with Nagiko in *The Pillow Book*, a movie she thought a *parfait mélange* of classical Japanese, modern Chinese, and Western film images. She craved difference, loathed diffidence. When she squeezed the bulb of the pipette, she wanted all those café eyes upon her, without their understanding that it was *only* this effect she desired to achieve.

This affectation had been spurious, but the longer it persisted the more she understood it would become part of her. It was her hope that over time she would no longer remember its provenance, that she would subscribe to the Theory of Obscurity.

The early morning clientele were different from those come evening. The garments worn, the conversation, the sense of purpose were transformed by the hours, as if the incremental movements of the minute hand on the white-faced clock over the counter transformed the customers, changing them from Technicolor to monochrome just as day turned towards night.

Imogen didn't consider herself a night or a day creature, yet this wasn't quite the case. For her, *day* was London and *night* was Paris. Living in a different city fluctuated her on/off switch. She could reinvent herself in a locale where the inhabitants didn't know her – or, perhaps more diligently, she could *be* herself; the reinvention a sloughing of conformity, convention and expectancy. The clean slate of potential excited her. Yet at the same time, she craved someone to share it with – if it were only *her* who noticed the change then for others there was no change.

It was with this in mind that she determined to locate her silhouette – a man as shadowy as he were dark, a doppelgänger lover, who would cling in adulation and respect but who would not exist without her allowance of existence. Nervous and warm-hearted, she scanned the streets of Paris daily as she walked to her employment, knowing that the enormity of what she was hoping for would stymie any attempt to make contact.

At the perfumery she was treated with mild interest. Her Parisian colleagues found it uneasy acknowledging her obvious talent and background. They were civil, frequently charming, yet it was there that her otherness, her *outsiderness*, was most keenly felt. Having to exist in the real world pushed her fantasies to one side. Indeed, when working, Paris could be London could be Milan could be Ulan Batar. The mechanics of the 9 to 5 were static.

The escape – the sinuous merging of strangers on the street and the reality of her colleagues – came in the form of customers. Those who crossed the threshold of the establishment with its little bell – invited by the window display just as a fictional vampire required an invitation into a home – brokered temporary contracts with Imogen's knowledge and personality. Whilst the majority of these were female, some of whom hid their disdain lightly, on occasion the perfumery purchasers were male. Yet as her perfumery exclusively sold products for women, it was inevitably the case that – with some degree of attachment – each of these males were already *involved*. This was the catch-22 of potential relationships: should she break in order to rebuild?

Nevertheless, the perfumery was rife for sexual liaison; the atmosphere heady with erotic anticipation. Regardless of modern thought, the perfumes were intended to drive the male libido skywards. Fragrances were no longer required to mask the scent of decay but to advance the concept of youth. Feminists might argue that perfumes belittled women but Imogen believed that it empowered them. Without question, humanity's sole existence led to the power of the rut.

Heads colluded, bent over a scent. Close proximity inspired giddiness. Invariably she was required to proffer her own wrist, sample-sprayed, to ensure that the customer bore no tell-tale traces of his task. Noses twitched her way, sometimes touched. In the majority of cases this dance of the senses was as repugnant as it was sensual; like a prostitute, there could be no discernment. She took what arrived: the old men buying scent for younger girlfriends, the ugly men with bulbous noses hoping for a placation or a rekindling of a decayed marriage or failing love affair, the geeks believing themselves emboldened by entering a female domain in the hope that a fragrant gift might bring their counterparts closer. All of these were required to be discarded, even as the financial transaction veered towards the sexual, in deference to the one customer who would rise above the rest, who would recognise beneath the fabricated scent the aroma of Imogen's actual being; and who would repudiate all others in order to be with her.

Each of Imogen's days was spent in somnambulant reverie.

Her preconceived images of Paris bit the dust.

She saw few Citroen 2CVs. The car ceased production in 1990 and her celluloid experiences

overpopulated reality. Likewise the Peugeot 403
– so beloved by Columbo – barely scratched the
surface of the tarmac. Gitanes were outlawed
gypsies; Gainsbourg only an echo within his
daughter. The conformity of Western civilisation
fit over Paris and, despite attempts to shrug it off,
such tremulous vibrations created an embrace. Yet
nostalgia wasn't sufficient to halt time.

However, viewed through the glaze of
desperation, through the perfumery windows,
through the tepid shade of her sunglasses, and
from her garret apartment, Imogen perpetuated
her preferences, glamorised the unglamorous. As
though reading a novel from the page, she added
more than she detracted, and, in response, each
insight of each character became elevated beyond
their apparent normality. She wrote the book even
as she was reading it.

Even so, a hard edge of distance – whether
from a subliminal cultural barrier or from her
shell of Britishness – threatened to make her
impenetrable. If she were her own character in a
novel then she held no identification. Either way,
inside or out, she required a heart.

Let's give her one:

In London she was girly and affectionate, the
centre of a crowd of successful females who dated
and performed as though in a feel-good American
TV show. Warmth radiated, blended sunlight
from artificial light, imbued her coterie with smiles
and assurance. Imogen was the one turned to for

relationship advice, Imogen was the one turned to for practical advice, Imogen was the one turned to for sexual advice, Imogen was the one turned to.

"And then she said – "

Never a bitch nor a gossip.

Yet her personality bordered on homogeneity. Imogen lost herself within her friends' appreciation, chameleoned into who they wanted her to be. Some nights were spent crying uncontrollably, naked on the fifth floor of her glass-fronted apartment, a lupine howl at the glow which took a billion light-years to illuminate her slender figure from stars which were already dead.

There was much to be said for singularity, but occasionally it was the plural she craved. Yet whenever she met anyone, her well-meaning gaggle of friends provided abstract assistance, tainted her in the man's eyes before they had time to rove. She couldn't be herself within that group, its essence had imbued her too long, and she found it impossible to regain her independence.

All animals follow fight or flight and she flew to the city she knew from travel advertisements, movies, French lessons, and imagination. Hard yet fractured, fractured yet hard. Imogen is you and I and us all together: an everywoman of reticent possibilities. A hand held deep within the cookie jar.

Her heels click-clicked on the pavement. Her perfumery colleagues having abandoned the shop like water droplets after a splash – only to assimilate themselves the following morning. She held her head high: viewed the *boulangerie*, the *boucherie*, the *charcuterie*, the *laverie automatique*, the *épicerie*, drinking in their reality and their fantasy. Shopkeepers returned her gaze, reeling her into the store as a fisherman might tease a catch; but the acrid smell of the *poissonnerie* scurried her feet, and head down she regarded the pavement – rooted by concrete.

Heels, bare legs, mid-length black skirt, white blouse, thin black summer jacket: conformity came easy.

Click-clack-click-clack.

Black birds circled the air, signalling a vortex.

Her French – both spoken and listening – was good, but submerged in a crowd voices became indistinct and set the world on a foreign keel. The busiest part of her walk was a cut through a modern shopping centre, where voices, images, and the near-absence of odours, surrounded her. Like immersion in water, snatches of conversation peripherated around her head, a bubblebath of sonic echoes. It was in these moments that she felt the most dangerous. As though she were a spy in the midst. As though she could do anything she chose.

A group of five Algerian youths regarded her askance; leaning on each other like a pack of cards. Two middle-class women – viewed through her British sensibility – ran poodles off leads *oohing* and *aahing* for unknown purpose. A collection of school children of both sexes, still in uniform, hung around an electronics store, each of their faces device-illuminated. A solitary man, grey overcoat, worn shoes, occupied a bench in the middle of the centre; resembling a stone in a river, the crowd surging by with no more thought than water has for rock.

Clack-click-clack-click.

The day had been uneventful. The usual collage.

Imogen emerged from the shopping centre and swung a right. Parkland was ahead: a green expanse. She skirted the perimeter, one short cut too many. Trees lined the avenue like spectators at a wedding as she walked down the aisle. A dart of movement awry: a squirrel? She breathed and took in the scent of cut grass, a *coup de grace* for her senses. She slipped off the black jacket and the fine blond hairs on her arms quivered attentively. Her purse was in her pocket. The other pocket held a lipstick and perfume. Jean. Paul. Gaultier. She rarely carried a handbag, a bag of any description. In London she had made a fetish of it – and if there was one peccadillo she carried across the water it was this one.

Yet it hadn't been across the water, had it? Imogen had not found her way to Paris via the air or sea but through the intestinal tube which was the Chunnel. She had found the experience alarming: normal and abnormal. Entering the tunnel was akin to falling asleep, awakening in the new air of her destination, which only felt fresh due to the human contrivance of geography. In essence, everywhere was the same, boundaries were manmade. Yet, having been carried under the water, it was also clear how determined

14

populations were to define their otherness; regardless of brand familiarity or product homogenisation. It had been made instantly obvious to her that she was in France: all those telltale subtleties. It led her to wonder why the country's proximity did not cause them to blend together in syncopation.

Dogs barked across the parkland. Cars braked and stilled. Planes tracked the skyline, chemtrails whitening. Noise funnelled through the tree line accompanied by a sudden wind which made Imogen consider replacing her jacket. Then she decided: *I will leave it off no matter how cold it gets.* Once she defined convention, now she defied it.

Another turn, the park to her rear. A line of tall buildings replacing the trees. At the end of the short lane, her boarding house peeked around the corner. She saw in it a liberation but also a harness. Once inside, the opportunities of the world were closed to her. The fantasy of finding the male that she longed for would be obliterated within those four walls. Whereas the exactitude of her address confirmed she had made the leap, its very confines were in themselves a prison. But where could one spend twenty-four hours a day in the fringes of hedonistic pleasure?

We each had to eat, sleep, defecate, work, shop.

Click-click-clack-clack.

Imogen reached the door of the boarding house. The café downstairs was lit dim, the evening clientele hunched over shot glasses making rapid conversation. She nodded to the concierge – a term Imogen preferred to *landlady* although she wasn't aware how the woman defined herself – and headed, head down, up the stairs at the rear to her room.

Once inside she divested herself of clothing and ran a bath. Waiting for the water's sonic frequency to indicate her desired depth, she reclined on the quilted bedspread and felt the almost-bubblewrap pockets of air punctuate spaces around her skin. Closing her eyes, she slipped into waking dream.

The men wore plague masks of the bird beak fashion, together with drab ankle-length grey coats, boots, gloves, and wide-brimmed hats. She could smell lavender from crushed flowers pressed into the nose cone. They pirouetted around the bed; with each turn, worn fingers unbuttoned their garments, until all that was left were the masks and their penises swirled like guy ropes in a sea breeze and they spun faster becoming smaller before they winked out of existence.

She woke, startled.

The bath water played echo music and Imogen rose from the bed shedding the vestiges of the dream. The air rippled in front of her, a smudged eye floater effect. Entering the bathroom steam depicted the heart she had drawn with her finger on the glass-fronted cabinet the previous day. The natural oil on her skin causing the steam to coalesce at a different temperature. She wiped it from the cool surface. In the bath, the water was of sufficient depth for her needs and she turned off the tap. Then wondered how long she had slept.

She eased herself beneath the water, the heat invading the spaces within her body.

Under water she opened her eyes. A film clung through surface tension. She replayed her dream against the faux bubble, her body completely still so as not to ripple the illusion.

After a while, her right hand snaked between her legs and the water frothed as the tide came in. A gratuitous frenzy.

She dressed: t-shirt and jeans. Pop socks and comfortable shoes.

In the café, they served food together with alcohol. She ordered chicken and fries, a traditional *fayre* marred by repetition throughout the known world. The chicken was dressed in its skin: a golden-fleeced thigh. Salad and sauces arrived in separate containers. She cut the chicken, noticed how the smell prescribed the flavour. As the knife pierced the meat, heads were raised above shot glasses. She had changed the room's ambience.

She usually ate here, in the café, a semi-home. Outside the boarding house, the romantic restaurants were not designed for sole diners. There her singularity would highlight an absent shadow.

Waiters would become too attentive – whether from pity or lust. She would feel diminutive there, her Englishness worn on the outside rather than the inside. Here at least she could gorge on *le poulet* and receive admiring looks from clientele who knew what a hearty meal meant. When she crunched lettuce they returned to their discussions.

These mostly elderly gentlemen could have been but were not Camus or Sartre or Godard or Cocteau or Truffaut. They were the quiet underbelly, the workers without whom France would not exist. These men represented France as did Eiffel.

She cracked black pepper onto the chips, rustic in her mouth.

She wondered if the men at the tables, conspirators in discussion, were aware – or speculated – that she had masturbated.

She was a flattened surface waiting to take shape.

Chicken parts slid around her mouth, taking her throat. Cartoonish, she drew beak-masks on the clientele in the charcoal gaze of her mind's eye. Unseen they were more romantic, but also less garrulous, losing the edges of their definition. She removed their masks, replaced them on the room's few women. Yvette, cradling a drink she had poured for herself at the bar, became a swan from an ugly duckling. Imogen dismissed the thought. It was not her place to judge: she had spent her lifetime in avoidance. It was better to exist within a splendid world without undermining or soiling it. She removed the masks from the other women. Then she did the only thing possible.

She imagined the mask on herself.

The scent of lavender rose to her nostrils. Plague doctors considered the disease carried through smell in the generations before germ knowledge. Lavender overpowered her food, the warm hotness of the chicken, the fresh tomato and cucumber concoction, the potato sleeping-bag of the fries, these were subsumed by the sickly. She found herself involuntarily reaching for her face, scrabbling for the sides of a mask which weren't there. Her stomach jerked: once, twice.

Unbeknownst to the room which continued without her, sweat dampened her shaved armpits, ridged her forehead like the tentative senses of trapdoor spiders. She remembered the Fontana cover of an Agatha Christie novel which had terrorised her as a child: *Appointment with Death*. Again: a dramatic sense of something on her face. Bile rose to the back of her throat, as bile will. She bit down on her teeth, a potential oxymoron. Then regained herself, breathed deeply – *one, two* – relaxed. The shell of nightmare split sideways and halved at her feet. She wondered what had created the sensation.

Was it the duration of time in Paris?

Had magic entered her life?

Should she be uneasy or frankly terrified?

Imogen moved her clean plate to one side. She beckoned to Yvette who fetched her usual glass of mineral water with xenophobic distrust.

Bubbles cleared her palate. She rose as if finishing a performance; scratching her kneecap in a bow. A glance at the stairwell leading to her room signalled the termination of her evening. She looked at herself without mirrors. It should be *carpe diem* not *crap diem*.

Outside beckoned like holes in a bowling ball.

One two three.

She turned on a heel and exited the café. Enveloped herself within night.

Imogen walked in reverse, a negative image of her return from work. Sssh-Sssh-Sssh-Sssh. Her trainers scuffed pavement.

The park was inky at the end of the lane. Treetops smudged into the black skyline, indiscernible façades. Blackbirds slept in hidey holes. In the silence, sound was magnified. A moped exhausted its way towards her, pootled to distance. The wind rustled leaves as if shopping with plastic bags. She kept her gaze focussed on the park, on its vortex of opportunity. Once inside, she leant backwards against a tree, the bark imprinting her skin. Imogen imagined remaining still, her flesh coalescing against the knuckled exterior, until she grew to be part of the tree and would have to be cut sideways in order for her age to be determined.

Shapes flew before her eyes. An acrid tang.

She walked from the tree, ashamed for her reverie to be dog-torn and wild.

Imogen continued walking in sight of the perimeter; as though there were a stick pushed into the soft earth at the centre of the park and she were tied to a rope, she made her circumference. This – she thought – is my domain. She imagined males of all ages shapes and sizes present in the dark, awaiting her, awaiting. She would dance with their minds, gorge herself, their faces gleeful with salient drip.

She shook off the images. Paris was inside her. If she were going to cheat, it would be with the one true only.

Somewhere in the distance, skateboards rolled against pavement, an inexorable thunderous rumble.

Moonbeams spotlit leafy gaps. She ran from one to the other: a toe here, a toe there. She felt no more than her years. She stopped. She needed a missing hand. She remembered her father making paperchain dolls, each linked by fingers and foot, a succession of Siamese twins. This she was lacking.

The entrance yawned before her, golden teeth of lit buildings beckoned Imogen to exit the maw. She had gone full circle. Another day she might return to the shop, view that sensuous façade from the benefit of night, imagine herself there twelve hours hence, unfold the powerplay. But tonight wasn't the night for familiars. Tonight was the night for strangers.

She stepped lightly in the direction of her dwelling. A man stood on the corner, cigarette glow devilling his mouth. He nodded. Pulled down his homburg. He was fifty, if but a day. Gray suit. Totally Gray. Imogen allowed herself a smile. At the next corner she halted, pushed her hands downwards like knitting needles into the pockets of her dress and waited. Once he moved, she did too.

Expectation scurried her. She remembered days of milk bowls and metal spoons. His image drew a memory to her somewhere. Skipping rope burned in her hands. She counted quietly, under her breath. Measured the distance between them and kept it. Sssh-Sssh-Sssh-Sssh. She couldn't have followed in daylight, under the forever presence of the sun, the open spaces, the necklines. She was absorbed by the dark, subsumed and spat. In her reverse role she imagined anything was possible.

Permissible.

The cum-smell of damp laundry clung to the air. A child's balloon contained the night. She was a pixie in a sequined dress. Words assaulted her. She thought of *Midnight In Paris* and the luxuries it contained. The abandonment. The falling away of the outer world. She shadowed the man. Under night's glare she *became* his shadow. When he raised an arm to scratch the side of his face she reciprocated. She bent her legs emulating the heaviness of his walk. She didn't look back. She didn't look back.

The mirage stopped as he entered a bar. For a moment his arm remained outstretched, Imogen believed in a heartbeat that he held the door for her passage; but the illusion dispersed. Someone left the bar. Sadness mingled with excitement. He had passed on the baton. Simply passed on the baton.

The new man was older. Mid-seventies. He wore a thick coat despite the day; held the form of a cylinder. She changed her gait to his, frequently rubbed her fingers against the underside of her nose. She returned in the direction she had come. She hugged brick. She bent to tie a shoe-lace in her flats. She saw him give a quick left to right glance at a nondescript building just a few hundred yards from her lodgings. Lit buttons, a rectangle of pushable white squares, bore numbers no names. She had heard of such places. Her mark had entered a brothel.

Imogen retreated fifteen steps. She became wary of remaining on the corner just as a smile played at the sides of her lips. She had entered a dangerous game. Would it be here she would seek fulfilment. A *belle de nuit?*

The door opened and she followed a youth, boyish, good looks with a limp. She imagined the irony. He walked briskly, from Rue to Rue. He walked as though he were escaping, *had* escaped. He walked like a man with no burden.

And so Imogen continued. A zig-zag through her neighbourhood. From one false trail to another. Night bore on. Opportunities lessened. She steeled herself to sleeping outside. Imagined that unless she found a man who was destined to room at her own establishment, she might never find her way home. *I will stick to the game*, she thought; until reality forced her backwards.

The milk hung at the point of departure, then was sucked back into the pipette.

She threatened it with hot coffee. Steam fluctuated the milky pulse.

Morning dragged realism with it. A drudge was a drudge was a drudge. She found her language falling away, reduced to pleasantries and essentials. Even in the shop her mind couldn't wander. She sought the vastness of the sky. A group of women spoke too quickly, interrogating her French. She had to call Camille in a pique of embarrassment, and when they all laughed there was the sense of collusion.

At lunch – the hardened sides of her baguette – cut her mouth.

Cheese thinned.

Tomatoes sogged.

The ham was richer than she found back home.

Home. She decided not to consider this. Imogen forced herself into the present.

At the fountain, she crossed her legs on a bench. Leant back, arms outstretched, her wrists twisted like a resting puppet. Self-assured. Water droplets blew her way. A light facial. The sun was yellow paper screwed into a ball and thrown into the sky where it touched the stars and torched itself. Imogen wanted to be torched whilst she touched herself. She longed for an inverse world.

Passion awoke.

The afternoon was interminable. A trap was a trap was a trap.

She refreshed her make-up in the toilet. Puckered.

A few of the girls were going on elsewhere. She was reminded it was Friday. She shook her head: dispelled an evening of cigarettes, dancing and men. Imogen desired to prey solitary. She had too long been caught in the gaggle, unable to extricate her personality from the gang. But what destination could be visited solo? She scanned listings in *La Monde*, settled for Bacon.

She was going to make an exhibition of herself.

Dinner was a slice of pizza from a pop-up stall. Imogen stood beside a man in a white sailor suit whose earphones sounded like her grandfather tinkering with his wireless. Nearby, a woman scraped dog's mess from the heel of her shoe. Another woman with pink hair and multi-coloured fingernails leered into the face of her lover. Imogen thought piercings. Imogen thought pain. One of the woman's tattoos fell from her leg and onto the pavement, peeled away with the insincerity of a drunk.

You can do better than that.

The entrance to the gallery was ancient, the inside as modern as her. Lamb dressed as mutton. She passed over her euros and wished they were francs. Inside, wall arrows suggested a presence. She moved from one room to another: stood, sat, leant with her head on one side. All the distorted faces. All the distorted faces which depicted the truth. Nothing was so clear as interpretation.

She became aware of a presence beside her.

Later she might claim she knew this was François. It is easy to flirt with hindsight.

He moved as she had done the previous evening, with the barest trace of shadow.

She completed a circuit, mirrored him.

Archetypically handsome with a broken nose.

He would catch her if she fell: from here, from her apartment window, from the Eiffel Tower. He would be there in an instant.

Imogen envisaged the terrain. Moist land.

She played on her English. Stubbed her toe. *Shit.*

He looked.

She sat on a low bench before a matador triptych, eased off her right heel, massaged a stockinged foot.

The bench groaned as he sat down beside her.

The washing machine inside her head stopped.

Imogen considered ten don'ts for honeymooners.

Bonsoir?

There it was: a question.

Hold that trapped bird.

Imogen waved a curve of hair from across one eye. *Bonsoir,* she answered.

He talked to her of Bacon but all she could think about was pork.

At least ten, perhaps fifteen years older. Cured.

Something willed within her. A time. And a place. For this.

Imogen swelled with grapefruit cut to a pink centre, the hexagonal, Europe in autumn, a considered kiss, wood grain, the light inside a night-bus, sherbet paper, a select establishment on a clock face, baize, a *something awaits you at the post office*, hands falling from treacle, the certainty of a numbered book.

The look he gave her was extraordinary.

Space poured between them.

She made her excuses and left.

Cool night air brittled Imogen's exterior. She watched the entrance to the gallery.

She considered: an entrance is an exit is an entrance is an exit.

A vein throbbed deep inside her perineum.

A drum beat.

What the fuck am I doing?

Her friends in England, downing shots in rowdy nightclubs, pushing hands away with hands, their skirts riding up their thighs, ambivalent in her absence.

It all comes down to the rut.

She remembers: childhood books with bears and kangaroos, a boatful of kids, a burning house, one two three investigators, captured animals, the call of the wild, girls straddling giant guns whilst tennis rackets replaced heads. *I want it now.* She subsumes herself in literature.

She dismisses the shade of those greyhounds.

He is there. He leaves the gallery as though a die shaken onto a poker table. She watches him look from left to right. He checks his watch. He runs fingers through his hair. It had taken him thirty minutes to even consider looking.

She considers he isn't looking.

He is almost beyond time when she starts to follow.

Night closes in like cinema curtains over credits, the moon bleeding through cotton wings, the urgency of message.

Imogen stands. She is the drip at the tip of the pipette. She wonders if she were missed at the boarding house. Whether the crisp skin of a chicken awaited her. She considers her life from moment to moment. Those fragile beneficiaries. Is this the change she has been looking for inside of the change that she sought?

There is further closure, her thoughts wrapped around. Blinkered. Focussed. No soft sole tonight. Bare ankles mean adventure. Shoe leather chafes. She cuts a dashing figure. Careful of those steps! She ascends to the sidewalk, loses him in a thinning crowd, watches him resurface, considers a conflagration of ambulances.

She shakes her head. *What is it with that?* Distance lends enchantment. She decides to summarise in one hundred and ten words.

I was a traveller in an antique land, enticed by perfumery into the exotic. I abandoned myself to chance which is much different to fate. Whim and whimsy travel hand in hand. Once there were victims. Is it always hard being on the outside of the door? To reinvent myself I must be an inventor. Somewhere I lost the patent. On the other side of the ocean a sliver of me remains. Here I am. Brevity is key. Brevity and substance. If he sees me if he sees me if he sees me. He will know. I am unsure of the consequences of throwing myself into a love from which I am aware I will never recover. Wish-fulfilment. Be careful what you wish for over and above your word count.

Imogen slips sideways into the gutter.

He walks buoyant, as though carried on the cool night air which smells of discothèque bouquets. She is a seal in the wake of a speedboat, spume in her face and the originator of the species. As she walks she finds herself being stripped away, temporary transfers peeling from her skin. She is raw. An uncertainty. The point of darkness at the end of the cone of light. There is an unravelling, a blossoming of desire; although for what she cannot say. Could it be the fate of the hunt? Has the nebulous destiny she has craved decided to lay itself at her feet?

She turns at the corner and finds he has stopped.

He is not looking at her.

She follows his gaze over the skyline. Night has been thrown like a rug over grass. A warm woollen scent hangs in her nostrils. From some of the buildings, the heat of the day drifts skywards in an almost visible embrace. She clutches herself. The serrated spikes of pigeon barriers punctuate clouds. The city is filled with harsh realities. In her head she hears a *Delicatessen*-esque squeaking of bedsprings. Everyone is fucking except her. Something melts. A sense of urgency is carried on the breeze, as though a dog has sighted a deer. A flash sparks at the man's mouth and Imogen realises a cigarette is lit. He shakes his right hand, as though disposing of gum. Then walks.

Imogen waits. Her heart decides before her head. She walks quickly to the spent match, crouches and retrieves it with the fingers of her right hand. Looking from side to side she lifts up the bottom of her t-shirt and pushes the head against her skin. The heat has dissipated. It is barely a remembered glow. Yet her muscles clench and upon removing the match she finds some discolouration, a mark.

She wonders what the man might think of that. He is almost out of sight. As the distance increases, she becomes shocked by her actions, fearful of observance. What if Nicolette from the perfumery had witnessed this? Out on the arm of some boy. There would be no going back. She feels sickened, bruised by circumstance. A silken thread, sticky like spit, stretches from her to the man; she worries it might lapse. Slowly, regaining herself, reassembling, she continues to walk. And with every step her cunt hardens in resolve.

Then.

She is almost running.

Then.

She runs.

Her heels twist like giraffes.

Her ankles threaten to break.

She has lost sight of him. She remembers that *Bonsoir.* That delirious accent. There is a gymnast inside her with elasticated hands. She buckles in thrust. Her mind crowds. She is drawn in crayon and erased. Over and again. A late night supermarket illumines like a hotel at the end of the world, like it houses a sun. She scribbles over her face. She is a train, a thunderous locomotive without sound. She is burnt celluloid. She is alchemy.

And then...and with such a suddenness...with the slam of a door...he is gone.

She stops, violently, as though connecting with an invisible wall. *What is it Simon?* A voice sounds nearby. A girl steps out of shadow, languidly draped over her boyfriend. Imogen watches the girl click her fingers. She regards her own head as it drops to the floor.

Sunlight watches her.

Imogen wakes. She rests in her garret room. She remembers the couple, one arm over one shoulder one arm over another. She gave directions. She recalls reproach at the entrance to her lodgings, her landlady's grimace. She starts. But it is Saturday. The shop is open at the weekends but not staffed by regulars. Students from one of the colleges, those invested with perfumery-interests, those wearing whale masks dancing jitterbugs, these trainees begging free samples who clock out in the evening with their wrists weighed with scent, they take control at the weekend. She visited it once, incognito, her face to the glass, curious at the usurpers. She saw but a faint reflection of herself.

She stands naked. She walks to the bathroom as though on cobblestones, as though on crippled feet. Running the shower relieves tension. Perhaps she has been alone too long. Flaky reminiscence. Perhaps she should return to England and rejoin her friends with their routines and rituals. She spits down the plughole, a perfect shot from her height. Shower gel a slow trickle across her curves. She tips her head back, her eyes water. Her hair hangs behind her like foliage, like vines draped beneath a fall. Something is inside her. Something she cannot shake no matter that she might return to England. If she were to roll a die it would stop on an edge. If she were to flip a coin it would catch in the air. She cannot describe it to herself. Ordinary words are lacking. Fate. Love. They are meaningless to the tumult. All she knows is that Paris – and the man – are her undoing.

The shower gel is viscous between her fingers.

She steps out. Dries. Allows a butterfly touch.

She wonders what became of the boy and the girl. She is glad that they weren't the gendarmerie with their blank manga deer logo and their deep-blue uniforms with those hat-box-hats bearing sugar-icing thread. She has always crumpled under authority. Presumed herself guilty before being proven innocent. Once at school, with the details of the incident forgotten, she remembers a teacher moving from face to face – *was it you? was it you? was it you?* – moving onwards after each question until stopping at Imogen and repeating the question twice, before eventually continuing with a look intimating she knew it was her – even though Imogen equally knew that it wasn't.

Where was the sense in that?

At the breakfast table she realised her pipette was upstairs.

Those regulars – she was sure – having known of her nocturnal dilemma – were now committed to believing she was one of them. She pulled a croissant into two pieces, buttered it. Bread stuck to the knife and without a glance she slipped it into her mouth. The doughy texture, the soft butter, the underside of the blade: a culmination of senses. She imagined the scene in the perfumery: the bread the base note, the blade the top note, the butter the theme. It would be a perfume for a unique and irreplaceable being.

She didn't know what to do with the day.

Imogen ate the croissant. She would head out to Montmartre. She would visit the Basilica of the Sacré-Cœur.

She dressed conservatively: pumps, jeans, t-shirt, cardigan. She left her lodgings allowing the door to swing shut behind her. Paris was wet-fresh, it had rained under the night. Steam rose as curlicues, like curlews disturbed by a fox. It had reinvented itself, the rain resembling vermix covering a newborn. Imogen had the sensation of the city slipping from the sky's vulva, falling fully formed and beautiful whilst she had slept.

She made her way to Jules Joffrin and rode the Montmartrobus stopping at the Place du Tertre.

It was difficult to disengage from history. She stood at the entrance, leaflet in hand. She disputed *from the dawn of time* but accepted the validity of the Gaul druids, the Roman temples dedicated to Mars and Mercury, the Church of St Peter, the Royal Abbey, and the Sacré-Cœur Basilica itself with its interactive thumbnails.

Religion sank her boats but the artifice of religion, the sexual power of monuments, these were of interest. She walked in the footsteps of others: gazing up, down, across. She lost herself in the fragility of tourism. In the corner of her vision, in the corner of her mind, she looked for him, vainly. She considered double meaning. The impossibility of perfection. But he did not ride resplendent nor descend from the heavens. And neither did the man that the religious came to see.

Her stomach rippled under her fingertips. She couldn't recall the food she ate. In the gleaming white toilets she tumbled out, barely in time, took tiny sips from a water bottle. Evian. When she stood, her head cleared dizzy, took upon itself to remind her who she was. She sat again: another swift movement. She wondered how many others had occupied the cubicle just as she, surrounded by the magnificence of the Basilica, just as they were consumed by base body needs. There was an immediacy to her existence – at that exact point – which thrilled her. Coughing, she cleared herself again.

Leaving the cubicle coincided with a tour party. She tagged along, unpaid. A man brushed against her elbow, glanced at her under tight-wired hair. She considered him swarthy – an expression she used to read in cheap novels and had never transferred to real life. When he smiled, his teeth were domestic-appliance white. Imogen returned it as a placebo, a platitude. They walked adjacent in silence, the guide intoning this and that. She considered how easy it might be to break free and fuck him, find some alcove and slip out of her jeans, loosen his and release his heat. All men were ready for that, weren't they? All men weren't aware that women were. The thought of it disgusted her.

She rode the cable car to Anvers and took the metro from there. Along the Seine, she swung her arms back and forth as she walked in tune to the *Umbrellas of Cherbourg*. Stopping for a glacé, she pushed the cold stem against both lips, then bore a hole in the centre with her tongue. On tiptoe, against some bridge or another, with her heels rising from her shoes as though elevated, she watched boats file past in an unexpected parade. Arms waved towards her, five fingered salutations. She waved back, blew cold kisses, pressed herself viscerally against stone.

The world was on her side.

All that was required was to wait. She knew with the certainty of cotton-wool that the man would return. She needn't chase any longer. Her compass would spin in his presence and with that reaction there would be an equal and opposite reaction. He would taste her as she spoke, touch her as she smelt, see her as an amalgam of five.

So Imogen heartened herself by the day.

Sunday passed in a solipsistic reverie whereupon she didn't leave her bed but waited with fingers pressed tight for the almost inevitable calling at her window.

When he didn't materialise, she forced herself through work Monday to Friday, paving the way for karma by being overly solicitous to the darkened hags in their widow's black who bought lavender and hissed at her with parma violet breath; with the bright-white-bloused architects from across the rue who looked down their noses at both staff and product with a gleam for both; with the men chasing forgotten anniversaries with flowers in hand or to be purchased later; with teenagers discovering their sexuality.

One lunch break she journeyed to the *pharmacie* and bought a dozen pipettes. That morning she had volunteered for stock check, and that afternoon – in the back of the store, darkened by boxes head height – she counted and miscalculated, broke a handful of seals, secreted a nipple-full of perfume from each of the brands via the pipette into a cylindrical tube for urine samples. With fist clenched she shook the concoction. Upon evening she doused herself gently. She was every girl, she was herself, she was bait.

She lingered where she had fallen.

Doors opened and closed like sphincters.

She examined the skin on the backs of her hands.

We are all artifice. What is in full sight merely hides what lies beneath the surface.

She no longer knew herself: this English girl who had travelled, who had wanted to be other, who was now tied to the certainty of the rut, who clawed at the evolutionary impulse. She wanted desolation, to be strewn across the pavement, her skin taut against kerb, her legs spread awaiting rain, an edifice tightened over the hole of a drum. She was elastic-wanton, needful and urgent. And with that drumming, that thrumming, she vibrated, she attuned her soul to the frequency of the universe, she emanated herself in waves.

And so, Imogen reasoned, it could be no other than that he would find her. And after twelve days, find her he did.

She was slouched on the corner. In one hand an orange Kwenchy Cup, the point of the straw poised to penetrate the seal. She wore a yellow skirt, wrapped ribbonlike around her thighs. Her white blouse revealed the shadow of her bra, reminiscent of a harness seen through water, a shopping trolley festooned with algae. Her feet were crossed at her heels. She might resemble Christ should she outstretch her hands and maybe it was this possibility which drew him into the late afternoon. She didn't notice the alcove from which he emerged, from where he had already been watching her, but then she saw him and her thoughts coalesced with each step.

My name is Imogen. I am a wildflower of uncertainty. I am to be budded by the gazelle of hope. I am a female Dionysius, a suitcase yet battered, a kaleidoscope of future and past. I am legion. I am wet. I am drinking life through a straw. I subsume. I will subjugate. I will turn on a penny and pirouette in a box. My name was Imogen. My mind is swept leaves: both an object in itself, and made from objects. Even those objects can be further defined. All that remains is definition.

She shook her head when he offered a cigarette.

"English, no?" He dragged. "*Shit* not *merde*. It was a giveaway."

He has a nonchalance of being, an easy sexuality. *This is a man*, Imogen thinks, *who has fucked*. One of the few to have done so. She lowers her eyelids, unsure if she is feigning or genuinely embarrassed to find him, now, here.

She sees his thumb flip the side of the cigarette, watches ash float like parachutists to the ground. Within everything there is beauty.

When she gazes upwards she cannot avoid his eyes. She says nothing. She thinks of how she might mention Bacon, of life's swerve, of the underside of faces, about how art is the most dangerous of all. Yet these thoughts are tidal-swept, redundant. She has sought him out: he realises this. He understands the heat in her cunt.

His fingers reach, brush a stray hair from her forehead. *Gosh!* she thinks, *a clichéd romance*. Then she captures his finger, the warmth in her grip, before returning it. That simple touch infers *I want all of you*.

He grinds out the cigarette against the brick of the wall. She notices that the spot is well-marked, wonders how many others have stood waiting for this. For a moment a chill runs up her back, perfection in ice-shoes. Then he says, "Before this happens, I will show you my Paris."

She turns, his hand finds her shoulder, guides her.

He demonstrates the breadth of the city.

This hamburger joint on Place Blanche is the Brasserie Cyrano. *It was here the surrealists dissected their days: the torments, frustrations, mundanity, corkscrewed through the eyes of those artists. Nearby,* Moulin Rouge *resonated with dancers on wood, an eclectic erotic impulse which – if he had a mind to it – Luis Buñuel might have connected to the drums of Calanda. Have you eaten? The food here is quick. Louis Aragon might not have approved.*

I'll take your hand.

Here, at 42 rue Fontaine, Breton lived for decades, assembling a collection of manuscripts, masks, drawings and objects. This apartment was the heart of the movement, much like the train station at Perpignan was Dali's universal centre. Long after Breton's death the contents were sold for 46 million euros. It couldn't be saved as a museum, although some might say that museum has been transferred worldwide.

My name is François.

Not dissimilar to Bacon, no?

We'll walk down this hill on Rue Notre Dame de Lorette then take Rue due Faubourg Montmartre. Here! The Boulevard Poissonnière.

Spin. Spin and tell me what you see.
Nothing?

Between Rue Vivienne and Rue Notre Dame des Victoires is the entrance to the Passage des Panoramas. *Take the passages further and into the* Galeries. *In the time of the surrealists, between the wars, these passages had been abandoned. They loved the empty shop windows with their redundant mannequins. With their poses.*

We'll turn off here, take a right down Boulevard Bonne Nouvelle and walk to the Porte Saint Denis. Breton made this journey daily. He met Nadja here. The surrealists connected with these disconnected buildings, these half-ruins, this out-of-context architecture. You see how the ancient gate, devoid of its town walls, now sits anachronistically in chaos?

The surrealists themselves were objects out of time. Yet they couldn't exist nowadays. They had to be of their time in order to reflect. It is precisely the same with all geniuses. If you took Leonardo from 15th Century Italy you wouldn't have a Leonardo with any use. Genius has to offend and can only do so against existing culture.

Stop.

I kiss you here.

Imogen's lips oscillated.

Her head was on fire. She was a temporary topography of transparent arcs. Hedgehog quilted.

She was a jigsaw knocked from a table, reassembling before the floor.

François was every kind of right.

Again, on tiptoe. Again, brick.

She imagined herself an ocelot, sleek camouflaged chic.

She found him disengaging.

Let's descend, at the Strasbourg-Saint-Denis, and take the metro towards Porte d'Orleons. We rise to the Ile de la Cite. The Place Dauphine is a short walk from here. The truth is that Breton saw in this place an embodiment of the female sex. The Place Dauphine's triangular form, the slot, that divides it into two tree-covered pieces, all this looked to him like the sex of a woman. The two arms of the river Seine that join each other at the pointed western front of the island would be, in this optic, nothing else than the legs of the lady. There is an erotic magnetism at stake on Place Dauphine, which is so strong that people prefer to avoid it. It's actually one of the most beautiful and deserted squares in Paris.

Imogen transposed herself on the view. She grew fifty foot, settled on the Place Dauphine as though easing backwards in a bath. She paused. Then spread her legs to the avenues, raised her head as François – jaw agape – viewed her intimacy.

As the reverie ended she found herself blushing.

François watched her curiously.

"We make connections," he said, slowly, "we assume a consequence. But it is just as crazy to state that Tom & Jerry beget violence as it is to quote Breton that the simplest surrealist act would be to run down a street indiscriminately firing a gun, and then use that as the starting point for all assassins."

Imogen thought: *you are my assassin, you have fired my gun.*

François said: "Magritte is to have said that being a surrealist means barring from your mind all remembrance of what you have seen, and being always on the lookout for what has never been."

Imogen thought: *I have never been until you remembered what I had seen.*

François said: "I remember Camus who said 'we know the surrealist solution: concrete irrationality, objective risk'."

Imogen thought: *objectify my concrete thighs.*

François said: "Frida Kahlo said she never knew she was a surrealist until Andre Breton came to Mexico and told her she was."

Imogen took François' hands.

She held them to his lips.

"What remains," she said, "is silence."

Returning to her apartment she was aware of a buzzsaw, a guttural intonation, background discomfort. She knew it was the edge of reality, burring against fantasy with a firework frisson. She discarded preconceptions. Proximity to François obliterated anything exterior to the sphere. She could view any item: a packet of dry roasted peanuts, an adolescent in vogue, centuries delayed, two fresh cream strawberry and custard tarts, the tumescent root that hangs from the tree, a sideshow matinee, government papers, crime – and they were made manifest through the gauze of François.

Think first: the eggs of the rhino-bird, a Hiroshima cut-out, a watch running backwards, breasts with reddened – beaten – nipples, a cock, an afternoon wisely spent, time travel, surrealism.

Or on another day: the mechanics of dancing prevent the automata from taking the lead because, given Asimov's Three Laws, all they must accomplish is to follow.

She whispered in François' ear: *Unpeel me.*

When Imogen entered Paris she believed it the city of romance and love. Of starlit clichés. She had forgotten it was the birthplace of surrealism, that decadent non-necessity. Yet the two had merged with François, who sat astride her; his cock wedged against the succulence of her anus, as he pulled a string of sugarmice from the hollow between her thighs. These milky-white, baby-soft, luxuriant beads which laced lips. Each smooth body eked tiny breaths as it eased, as if Imogen herself were a sugarmouse and Paris a cunt. Illuminated follicles, sun-drenched night. François was solid: the corroding metal facade of Montparnasse Cemetery, where Sartre, the existentialist, decomposed. Imogen considered him now as she thought of herself: meaningless yet perfect. François slapped her from the reverie with cotton candy sentences. Her eyes widened, pupils' embryos in frogspawn.

François held a sugarmouse above his upturned head and lowered it into his mouth, sucking until disintegration from sodden string.

Imogen reached for the colossal. Fingerprint indentations on marbled frames. Canvasses fell into her, an immersion in art. Paint freckled her skin. François traced patterns with pencil and compass, created harsh lines against curves. A radiant link. Each touch resonated deep, indelibly fixed her in time and space. She wanted to touch herself, to caress her darkness, but François held her back; slipping fingers into the void. Imogen exploded warmth. Virulent foliage. Tiny animals ran through the underground, their eyes ablaze. François raised her. Her buttocks lifting from the damp polyurethane, sticky undergrowth. Air tingled, suffused with those emotions, with subtle balance. The space engorged.

Time stilled.

Imogen arced her back – an Arc de Triomphe. François' fingertips drove cars over her body, stylised tyretracks. *I am a milky way of you*, she hushed, *I am tempered flight.*

She watched François nod. His movements were slow, deliberate. Anticipation was a vibrating egg in the nest of a crow. She curled her toes, existed in her extremities. François stood, his cock unfurled like a tongue. She craved it as both moist length and rigid obelisk. A symbol and a statement. Reaching out her fingers, it fluttered under her touch, an engorged caterpillar awaiting butterfly transformation. She held it stiff, guided, expected.

Whilst outside the casement window, the city breathed luxuries and apartments, compartments compressed amid Parisian immigrants burnt with insolent heat. Stuttered sky blistered painted shavings falling as leaves; a twist of sycamore. The Eiffel Tower simultaneously a vulva and a penis, a metaphor for the bump and grind of the city, a synonym for a ménage à trois, that resonated through its traffic through bedsprings through the hindlegs of dogs through birdsong through the tumultuous waves of flushed toilets entering the sewer through categories of vegetables through peroxide Americans fanning themselves with guidemaps over cooling cups of coffee through crevices, through doors.

I am captured, Imogen breathed, her legs widening as the head of François' cock touched her, nudged her pudenda. *I am shame.*

François enlivened. As a wild thing he penetrated, a pig nosing for truffles. He filled her.

As a wild thing he ravaged. A tiny exploration. Imogen felt him.

A tremor coursed under the streets, buckling tarmac. Horns raided sunlight. Gargoyles tottered, claws of stone. François's length was to Imogen's depth. A concave opening, he placed fingers inside, extracted algorithms and hummingbirds. Porcelain cracked. Fenders steamed. Heat rose up beneath the city and lifted it skywards. Imogen sentenced a scream and it dropped, buildings fractured, brick dust flushed, pavements ran shadowed rivulets along their length like drunken stenographers. In the barbershops, haircuts cut askance.

Imogen tightened. François placed antique filigree nuances in her belly button. He fucked her hard. The nuances rattled. When he emptied, a knotted warmth shot forward and embedded in his forearm. Imogen leant up, her pelvic bone grinding against his member, released it with teeth, swallowed. The warmth journeyed to her heart. A calm veined bicycle track. The culmination of everything she had searched for.

It was thus how she imagined her descent; a gradual suicide into a faction of normalcy.